DEADLY DRAGON'S INTENSE INFATUATION

COMPANY 417 SHIFTERS SERIES

AMELIA WILSON

CONTENTS

I

I'm not supposed to be here.

That could be the theme of my life.

Mari isn't supposed to be here. What are you doing here, Mari? Why don't you go away, Mari? For God's sake, Mari, why do you always show up where you don't belong?

Okay, that's a little melodramatic. I don't want it to seem like people didn't love me or I was some sort of unwanted child. My parents love me as much as any parents love their children and always have. I have friends and a good job. I have a nice apartment in a safe neighborhood and a reliable car that is well-maintained and comfortable.

I have a good life.

The problem is, I have a penchant for showing up places I shouldn't be. Railroad tracks, abandoned mills, closed shopping malls, deep in the forest at night when wolves are hunting. Most of the aforementioned comments were a result of my parents having to once more rescue me from a precarious position because I decided to go somewhere I knew I wasn't supposed to go.

It's not my fault, really. I don't mean to get into trouble. I just get lost in my head a lot. I spend a lot of time with my head in the clouds, imagining myself as a warrior princess or a ship captain or a superhero or one of those kids who goes on adventures with talking animals. Most of the time I don't even decide to go somewhere I'm not supposed to, I just end up there because I'm caught up in a fantasy.

I wish I could say that I've gotten better as an adult, but I haven't. I'm still the same scatterbrained girl at twenty-five as I was at eleven and though I rarely get myself into the same kind of trouble I dd when a little girl, I still find myself neglecting chores or work because I'm daydreaming about riding a noble steed and leading my knights to victory or else rescuing my prince from the jaws of death or else sailing uncharted waters and discovering a new world.

Today is different.

Or rather, today is the same as it was when I was eleven and not like it is now that I'm twenty-five.

Today, I am definitely somewhere I don't belong.

I don't realize I don't belong here at first. There's a sign that says area closed, but I'm caught up in my head, so I don't register what it says until much later when the reason for the closure becomes apparent.

I enter the closed area of the forest because my current fantasy is that I'm a brave explorer in the Amazon Rainforest, studying and discovering new species. I am reading an account of Theodore Roosevelt's escapades in the rainforest and since I leave work early today, I decide to spend some time outside instead of going home and curling up with the book.

I intend to take a nice, leisurely stroll through the front part of the forest—the part with well-marked trails, public restrooms, and water fountains, but instead I let my imagination get the better of me and drive a good ten miles into the forest, past where cars are supposed to go even when there isn't a special closure in effect.

I remember patting myself on the back for getting the rugged four-by-four SUV instead of the comfortable little sedan when I make it to the end of the trail and only have to stop because I am surrounded by trees.

I don't regret the choice in automobiles necessarily, but I do wish I had exercised better judgment in its use. At the same time, if I'm going to make it out of this alive, I'll need every ounce of that off-road capability.

Apparently fire departments don't just put out fires. Would you believe that they actually stop fires sometimes?

Yep. I guess the local fire company is going to do a controlled burn of this area of the forest. It's something called a burn break. I'm not sure what that is, but I know it means they're going to set the part of the forest I'm currently huffing and puffing through on fire.

I try to call nine-one-one on my phone to sheepishly admit that I screwed up and ask them to please not burn me alive for my mistake, but I don't get to do that because there's no signal out here. So, instead, I have to try to run the god-knows-how-many miles back to my car, then drive the mile or so away that will take me out of the burn area.

I don't feel afraid. That's the strange part. I'm so caught up in my sense of adventure that my brain actually decides that this is just a fun part of the adventure and I almost enjoy myself as I pound my way back to my car.

Then I feel the wind from the helicopter and fear finally catches up to me.

I sprint toward my car, and I don't think to question the fact that I feel the wind from the helicopter but don't hear the sound of the engine. I feel the wind increase until its howl is so powerful that I can't hear anything over it.

God, please don't let them start the fire yet.

I burst through a clearing and cry out with relief. My car is right in front of me. I hop in the driver's seat and tear away the way I came, wheels spinning and screeching.

I breathe a sigh of relief and that's when logic reasserts itself and I start asking questions.

Why are they using a helicopter to start this fire?

What kind of helicopter doesn't make any noise?

I should just go home, but of course, I don't. As soon as I pass the sign that says, NO ACCESS: CONTROLLED BURN AREA, I turn left and take a little-used trail that leads to the top of a ridge from where I can overlook the entire burn area.

I am desperate now, not to get to safety, but to get to a vantage point where I can witness the burn. I guess that just shows how flighty I am. One day maybe I'll grow up, but that day clearly isn't today.

I make it to the top of the ridge and get out of my car just in time to see the first jet of flame shoot from the helicopter.

Except it's not a helicopter.

I can't believe what I'm seeing. My first thought is

that I'm unconscious somewhere in the woods. I've hit my head and I'm dreaming. There's no way this can be real.

But it is. It's impossible to believe, but it's as real as I am. I stare wide-eyed as another jet of flame ignites more trees in a precise line that extends in a roughly three-mile by three-hundred-yard arc that bisects the forest in between two low hills.

The machine responsible for this fire isn't a machine at all.

It's a dragon.

It flies with long wings that stretch at least two hundred feet across, creating the wind that I mistakenly assumed was rotor wash when I felt it earlier. It's emerald green and gold skin shimmers in the sun and as I watch, it releases another jet of flame that shoots almost a thousand feet down to the forest below with perfect precision.

I stare open-mouthed and for a brief, beautiful moment, I am that eleven-year-old girl again and absolutely anything is possible.

2

FLYNN

I love flying.

I suppose that comes as no surprise. I've not met a single dragon who doesn't love flying. Of course, I've met precious few dragons even in my long lifespan. There are few of us left and we keep ourselves well-hidden. When the rest of the shifter community comes out to humans, it is agreed among dragons we will remain secret. It is deemed—correctly, in my opinion—that humans will more easily accept animal shifters than dragon shifters. Perhaps it would help if other so-called mythical creatures existed as shifters, but it seems those legends—vampires, werewolves, minotaurs, centaurs, mermaids and the like—come about as a result of contact between humans and animal shifters in their half-shifted forms.

In any case, dragons remain hidden and the necessity of that means that we rarely get to enjoy our dragon nature. In fact, many dragons really do spend most of their time sleeping or hiding, hoping that one day they can awake to a world accepting of them and not one ruled by worry. The reality is most non-dragon shifters have never seen a dragon. We keep to ourselves in general and more now than ever before.

Most dragons hope for the day when we can be more open. They'll probably see that day come. Things are getting better slowly but surely. Still, they aren't there yet and I, like every other dragon shifter, am forced to remain in hiding like all the centuries before for my kind.

Dragon shifters live far longer than humans and far longer even than other shifters. I am old enough to remember the last of the true dragons—the full dragons and not the shifters. Even in the Middle Ages when I was born, there were very few of them left, and by the time Columbus encounters North America on his journey to the East Indies, there were no more.

The shifters remain and though we are few, we are enduring. At least, I believe we are. Like I said, we rarely encounter each other.

I put these thoughts from my mind and focus on enjoying the limited time I have to fly. The fire breathing part isn't so exciting to me. I know of dragons who enjoy being fire starters and spend a lot of time in secluded parts of the world starting brush fires, but for me, the joy is being able to soar through the sky. I turn and make a final pass to burn the last remaining stretch of trees in the burn area, and wonder if I can risk a higher flight, perhaps several thousand feet up, just enough to see all of the forest.

I decide against it. This area is remote, but not so remote that a fifty-yard-long dragon with a seventy-yard wingspan won't be spotted by commercial flights if I fly above the ring of low mountains that contain this forest.

I turn around and begin heading back to the ridge where I will shift. I land with a powerful beat of my wings and spend a moment sitting still in dragon form, taking one last breath of air to fill the senses that my human form will never experience.

Oh well. All good things come to an end. I shift back to human and turn to head down the hill where my car and my clothes wait.

I stop before I take a single step.

The woman stares at me wide-eyed and there's no question that she saw me. The shock in my face isn't that she saw me, but that I somehow missed her.

As soon as I think that thought, I know exactly why I missed her. Her car is parked behind the only three tall trees on this ridge and of course I couldn't smell her or the car over the scent of flame and burning conifers.

She is beautiful. I rarely notice a woman's appearance. A lifespan that is within shouting distance of a millennium has offered me the chance to see countless beautiful women, and as flippant as it seems, few are more beautiful than the last one or likely to be more beautiful than the next.

This woman might be the most beautiful I've ever seen in my life. Her hair shimmers like burnished copper in the sun and her skin is smooth and soft and flawless. Her features exhibit the kind of perfect symmetry rumored of Cleopatra. Her figure is the perfect type that legends attribute to Helen of Troy, and her full lips all but beg to be kissed.

One legendary attribute of dragons is true: we do love collecting pretty things.

This woman in front of me would be the crown jewel of any collection and I must, I will make her mine.

She blinks and quickly spins on her heels. "I—I'm sorry. I didn't mean, um..."

Her voice trails off and I realize I'm naked. I forget sometimes that I can't just be naked around humans. Shifters see each other naked all the time and it doesn't carry the same sexual connotation for us that it does for humans. We change size and shape regularly, so it's not practical for us to wear clothes all the time when they're only going to be ripped to shreds.

"I apologize," I say, "I wasn't expecting to see anyone. If you'll give me a moment, I'll retrieve my clothes from my car and dress."

"I'm sorry," she says again. "It's just... Oh my God! You're a dragon? I thought dragons didn't exist!"

I smile and say, "To my knowledge, the last of the true dragons died several hundred years ago, but half dragons still exist, what you would call dragon shifters."

"Oh my God!" she says again, her voice soft and reverent with wonder. "I—I just never imagined—I mean you have dreams when you're a little girl, but you never think—Oh my God, you were *flying!* And breathing fire and everything!"

My smile widens as I hear her talk. There is childlike wonder in her voice, and I am impressed that there is not the slightest hint of fear. Most humans view dragons with some measure of trepidation, understandable considering we're the size of a small office building when in dragon form.

Yet, she is unafraid.

I stare at her in wonder and then pause. It only just now occurs to me that she isn't supposed to be here.

"Why are you here?" I ask. "Did you not see the signs?"

She turns around and says, "I'm sorry. I did see them, I just—this is going to sound crazy, but I read them all but somehow it didn't make it to the part of my brain that would say, 'Oh hey, maybe you should listen to this sign and not go into the controlled burn area,' so I—Oh," she colors and I realize I'm still naked.

"I apologize," I say. "I'll be back in a moment."

I walk to my truck and retrieve my clothes. I dress quickly and return to the top of the hill. I look out over the fire and see it is dying down already, leaving a perfect strip of land that will contain no usable fuel when the Bureau of Land Management clears out the charred debris over the next few days. If a forest fire occurs, it will be contained to the uninhabited part of the forest and pose no danger to population centers.

"Let's get you home," I say. "Miss..."

"Mari," she says, "Mari Angeline."

I extend a hand and a bolt of electricity runs through me when she takes it. "Flynn," I reply. "Flynn Aodh."

"Flynn," she says and it's as though a choir of angels sing my name when it passes her lips.

3

I can't believe this.

I try to wrap my head around it, but I can't. There's an honest-to-God dragon shifter sitting on my couch across from me with just my coffee table between us.

At the moment, he doesn't look like a dragon at all. He looks like any other man. Okay, not any other man. He looks like what all men wished they looked like and what all women wished all men looked like, but still, only a man. The only hint that he's more than an ordinary man are his piercing eyes that seem to glow with the flame inside of him and the cultured, almost archaic way he speaks.

I invite him to follow me home and Mariculously he accepts. I learn that he works for the local fire company and when I ask if they know he's a dragon, he confirms they do but that no non-shifter does except for me. I promise to keep his secret safe and he smiles and says, "I trust you, Mari. There's no need to reassure me of what I already know."

A shiver runs through me when he says that, partly because of how it feels to hear him say he trusts me and partly because his voice just radiates power. I know there are legends that dragons can charm humans and impulsively, I ask him if he's charming me.

He laughs and says, "No, not at all. It's true that dragons can influence a human's will—most humans, at least—to a great degree, but I dislike that practice very much. In the old days, it was necessary when nearly even human who saw us felt a need to try to kill us. It was either kill every human we saw or use that influence. I don't use it at all except in moments of great necessity. Besides, I suspect that I couldn't charm you even if I wanted to. There are some women—and they are always women—who aren't susceptible to our charm. I haven't tried to charm you, but—"

"Can you?" I ask. "Can you try to charm me?" He shifts uncomfortably in his seat, and I say, "Just once, so I know for sure. Please, I need to know."

He stares directly at me, and his eyes bore into me as he says quietly, but commandingly, "No, you don't."

His tone causes me to shiver again, but I repeat, "Yes, I do."

"No," he says again, more sternly. "You don't."

I want nothing more than to throw myself at him and tear his clothes off, but I control myself and say, "Just one time Flynn. Please, so I'll know."

He smiles at me. "You are immune to charm."

"What?"

"I just charmed you," he replies. "I attempted to influence your will to decide you didn't need to know if I could charm you and I failed. You're insusceptible to my charm, just as I suspected."

"Oh good," I say. "Then I can do this."

I cross the distance between us, straddle his legs and kiss him hard. He stiffens in surprise at first, but quickly recovers, lifting me off of the couch and returning my kiss.

God, there's so much power in the man!

I don't do this.

I mean, I'm not a virgin but you wouldn't need all five fingers of your hand to count my sex partners. Hell, if people were only allotted fingers based on how many men I've been with, there would be a hell of a lot of poking and no writing or using tools.

I want him, though.

I'm living one of my fantasy books. Hell, I'm experiencing something far more exciting and romantic than one of my fantasy books! I don't know if he can read minds, but he carries me through the apartment and knows exactly where to go. In just a moment, we're in my bedroom. Once we're there, he demonstrates that he has use of all five fingers on both his hands because my clothes come off as if by some sorcery.

My hands don't work nearly as well, and I end up staring at this incredible creature as he slowly removes his clothing and looks at me like I'm something delicious and he's starving. My mind is always a million miles away but not now. Right now, it's very much in the present and right now, the present is completely and inexorably mired in the sight of his perfect body.

He's like something out of a fantasy.

I know I've said that before, but it's the thought that

keeps sticking in my head, like this is a dream and at any moment I might wake up.

I don't wake up, thankfully. Instead, something almost as Mariculous as Flynn's existence happens. I find myself in control of my body once more and though my mind is still fixated on the impossible attractiveness of this man, my hands remember to pull him close and my legs remember to wrap around his while my lips remember to kiss his ear and whisper softly, "Take me, Flynn Aodh."

It's as though all of the power Flynn is holding back is suddenly released all at once. He growls and thrusts into me and as soon as he thrusts into me, I feel as though I've been lifted above the ground and thrown violently back down only to be lifted again and carried to heights of sensation that shouldn't be possible.

None of this should be possible, but it is. Flynn drives into me with an intensity and fierceness that would frighten me if I didn't still feel that somehow, I was in control. Physically, I am as close to a passive participant as can be, but it still feels as though I am the one that drives our interaction and Flynn is only acting as I want him to act.

It's the strangest feeling to feel that even though I am being taken as though I belong to him, it seems more as though he is giving himself to me because he belongs to me. He holds my arms above my head with one hand and with his other strokes my clit while still thrusting into me and I writhe and cry out and twist in near-panic, but still I feel that he is mine as much or maybe even more than I am his.

Then he cries out and as soon as I feel his cock pulse inside me, my own climax hits like an avalanche and drives all thought from my mind. I'm aware that I am screaming and shuddering and he's moaning and thrusting into me, but the overwhelming feeling—the one that supsersedes all others—is that we are one.

We float above the world, safe and warm and content in each other's arms. The world remains below us, easily within reach should we want to return, but at the same time, it is as far away as we need it to be. There is only me. There is only Flynn.

We are one.

4

FLYNN

Mari

Her name sings in my ears as I lay awake next to her watching her breathe. At a certain age, all dragons lose the need for sleep. Most of us sleep out of boredom, actually, or when physically exhausted after a great deal of exertion. I don't suppose sleep is something I have required in many years. As I see this petite woman next to me, I know I will not sleep at all tonight but will spend the hours until she wakes just drinking in the sight of her.

We are obsessive, we dragons.

I understand this, and understanding my nature is probably the only thing that allows me to function in a world of humans. I know my needs, and my needs are far, far smaller than my desires. Nonetheless, I am a dragon and for a dragon, desire and need are often blurred.

I desire this woman.

The line between that desire and absolute, all-consuming need is very, very thin, so thin that knowledge of that line is not enough to inspire me to regard it.

Her body is perfect. She rests with one leg draped over my thigh and her arms curled up next to her shapely breasts in and almost protective way. She is right against my side, her face pressed against my ribs. One of my hands rests on her shoulder and the contrast between my form and hers is profound. My form speaks of physical strength.

There is elegance in my body, yes. Even the weakest of dragons not only appears in human form as the strongest of men but also the most agile and fluid. We are creatures that move with no wasted motion or effort. I stroke her shoulder softly and too late realize my mistake as she stirs. It is difficult to consider it a mistake, however, a moment later when her mouth moves on me.

Agile and fluid. Elegant. As she uses her mouth to bring me to a point of ecstasy, it occurs to me that no dragon will ever achieve her levels of those qualities while she's engaged this way with me. After, she snuggles again, and I force myself to sleep just to ensure that she can.

In the morning, we shower together, and I elicit a promise from her that I can visit her again after my shift with Company 417. The rest of the company works a schedule with four days at the station, eating and sleeping there as well and then three days off. They cycle through that so that all seven days there is a contingent ready to fight fires. I work a different schedule. I work five twelve hour shifts per week. I am a dragon shifter and I require the solitude that sleeping at the station prohibits.

I am fortunate that Company 417 is a company of shifters. Just as the bear is given time to hibernate (fortunately, bear shifters require only a week every three or four months) and the horse is never required to climb higher than three stories (we have a gorilla for that anyway); I am free to leave every night.

I don't need to work.

It's impossible to live for centuries without garnering unimaginable wealth. At least, it is impossible for a dragon shifter to live for centuries without garnering unimaginable wealth. We are attracted to gems and precious metals. We are attracted to beautiful things and beautiful things are valuable. Financial planners will tell you saving just a few hundred dollars a month for fifty years will make a person a millionaire when it comes time to retire.

Imagine what accumulating a little wealth regularly for centuries will do.

I have a bag of coins with a value in gold and silver of about half a million dollars. If I ever sell them, they will fetch nine or ten million dollars just because they were minted at the height of the Holy Roman Empire and some of them are the only fully intact examples of the coins in question. That bag is just one of many tucked away in a safe that is only one of many in various locations around the world.

But when a creature such as me lives for centuries, a lack of wealth (if it's even possible) isn't even important. Nor is fear for my safety or my health. The greatest threat facing a dragon is boredom. There are times pure ennui is so sharp it just consumes everything like a blanket thrown over me and suffocating me while it keeps me from any light at all.

I've heard rumors that the ancient dragons—the full dragons and not the half-dragons, us shifters—passed from this world due to this boredom. I have no trouble believing that. The ancient dragons lived impossible lifespans—many thousands of years—and just imagining the weight of those years is enough to make me shudder. No doubt when I am as ancient and world-weary, I too will choose to leave this world behind.

"Knight got your tongue?" a voice to my left calls to me.

I turn to Rory, who grins with the same mischievous look that he wears every time he makes that joke.

"Hilarious," I deadpan.

He bursts into laughter—excessively loud and boisterous as is usual for a bear-shifter—and I continue to deadpan, "The height of humor. Truly you are the king of improvisational comedy."

He lays a hand on my shoulder and says, "And you are the emperor of excessively extravagant expositions."

"Four e's," I reply in the same deadpan voice. "Your alliterative skills are impressive."

"I swear to God, if the two of you don't stop now, I'm going to tie both of your hands behind your backs and toss you into the middle of the next controlled burn," another voice says behind me.

I turn and grin at Stone—the company's horse shifter. "That wouldn't harm me, but I'm in favor of it if it will get Rory out of my ear."

"Well, a volcano for you, then," Stone says. "Anyway, chief wants to see both of you."

Callum isn't actually the chief. He's the company commander, but we call him chief because he's the most experienced firefighter in the department. He's a grizzled wolverine shifter with a handlebar mustache and a gruff expression that suits his shifter persona perfectly.

Rory and I report to him, and he says, "Fellas, I'm retiring next year. I wanted you to be the first to know. I'm nominating Rory for company commander and Flynn for deputy commander."

"Retiring?" Rory says, blinking. "I thought you were going to live forever."

"I am," Callum says, "I just can't stand seeing your ugly mugs anymore."

Rory laughs and says, "Well, sincerely man, I'm happy for you. What are you going to do?"

Callum shrugs. "Fish, probably. I'm a man of simple needs. Fast water and slow catfish."

"Will we still see you?" I ask.

It's a valid question. Some shifters—especially those who are solitary animals—retire and disappear from view.

"You'll still see me," Callum promises.

"Well then," I say. "Congratulations."

"Relax," he says, "Don't look so glum, it's not for a year."

I smile sadly. "A year is not as long for a dragon as it is for others."

He rolls his eyes, "Oh whatever, Ancient One. Just pretend to be happy like the rest of us normal people, okay?"

I grin and say, "For you, Callum, anything."

An hour later, that grin remains, because Mari texts me saying she has dinner waiting for me as soon as I can come over.

5

I masturbate in the shower.

I don't intend to. I'm just lost in my head. After a month with Finn, I'm still lost in my head all the time but instead of me losing myself in fanciful scenarios of adventure or imagining myself in some sword and sorcery plot line, I lose myself in thoughts about Finn. I'm certainly never going to imagine myself as a princess who needs to be rescued from a fire breathing dragon by a noble knight!

No. I spend all my time lost in my head thinking about this amazing boyfriend of mine, focusing on him and finding myself completely overcome by thoughts of him at all times. I think about his eyes. I think about how he speaks. I think about his face. I think about his muscular chest, and I think about his perfect form. I think about his strength, and I think about his voice.

And, of course, I think about his rather magnificent cock.

I mean, I don't want to turn our relationship into nothing more than sex. It's not like that at all. I mean, Finn knows Robert Louis Stevenson! Well, I guess *knew* is more appropriate. It's amazing to me all by itself to be able to have a conversation with a man about *Kidnapped, Treasure Island,* or the *Strange Case of Dr. Jekyll and Mr. Hyde.* There just aren't a lot of men out there who want to spend their time engaged in conversations like that. I get to have those conversations with Flynn and also conversations about what Stevenson thought of his own writing!

He is the most engaging man possible, and everything about him thrills me and fascinates me.

So, as I cry out, "Flynn! God, Flynn, fuck me!" against the stream of water flowing from the showerhead and thrust fingers into my pussy, I guess it's understandable that I masturbate even though I don't want to at the moment. This man is like the fulfilment of every dream in my entire life when it comes to romance and sexuality. Whether I intend to masturbate in the shower or not, the orgasm is extraordinary, and I feel weak-kneed and spent when it's over.

And that's the problem.

This is my second shower of the day and this one is the first step in me getting ready for when Flynn arrives after his shift. Since my plan is to engage right away in what I hope will be a very athletic bout of sex, being weak-kneed and spent is not where I want to be at all.

I groan and barely keep myself from letting out a stream of curses. I pull my fingers from my pussy and try to work myself back up to a heightened state of arousal. Hell, I'll be satisfied with just losing some of the sluggishness. I finally turn the water all the way to freezing and force myself to count to fifty before I get out of the shower, shivering and shaking but at least free from sluggishness.

I dress in a lacy black singlet which is intentionally see-through over my breasts and intentionally opaque in just enough of the crotch to cover my pussy. I wear matching black stockings and heels and head downstairs just in time to hear the doorbell ring.

I grin and open it and a few seconds later, I wonder how I could have worried at all about not wanting sex.

I definitely don't wonder anymore since at the moment my legs are in the air with my heels pointing skyward and Flynn is driving me to impossible levels of pleasure as he thrusts into me. Each time with him is still impossibly incredible and I wonder how it is that I still feel like an equal partner in this relationship when I am screaming and shuddering with an orgasm that makes the one I have in the shower feel almost pedestrian.

Perhaps it's the expression on his face that makes me feel this way. He seems to enjoy himself as much if not more than I do and though my body is spasming and shuddering uncontrollably, I feel somehow as though I'm the one dictating the action.

I don't dwell on this paradox anymore like I did the night before. I accept it as part of the wonderful things about this relationship.

"God, Flynn!" I cry out as he thrusts deeply into me.

He shifts his position to go even deeper and when he does, my hands slam against his ass and grip tightly as he drives my orgasm to even greater heights. God, how can he feel so good? It's impossible. I've never cum like this before.

I have, of course. The night before with Flynn, I came

like is. I came so hard I nearly passed out. This time, consciousness doesn't threaten to leave me but instead somehow intensifies along with my orgasm so that I am acutely aware of everything that is happening to me right now. I can feel each pulse of my climax as though it occurs in slow motion. Each contraction of each muscle rolls through me like a discrete thing, making my orgasm feel like a successive chain of orgasms beginning at my diaphragm and moving downward to my pussy and from there exploding up my spine and down my thighs.

I smell his strong scent as I bury my head in his shoulder and scream and though I scream, I hear every breath he takes as though they were my own. I taste the salt of his sweat as I kiss his ear and say, "Cum, Flynn. Cum inside me. Make me yours."

I am so glad to be his. I am so glad to have a relationship with such an incredible creature.

It occurs to me that I don't know for sure if we have a relationship. It's an odd thought and not an entirely welcome one given that it occurs while he's in the middle of gasping and shuddering over me while his cock is pulsing powerfully in my still-throbbing pussy, but it lingers in spite of the way I cry out and grip his arms tightly to try to steady my own shuddering body.

When I finally get a chance to speak, I say, "So what are we?"

He lifts himself up and asks, "What do you mean?"

"Are we in a relationship?" I ask, "Or are we just fucking each other?" I ask. "Either is fine, I just want to know."

He stares silently a moment and says, "We are one, Mari."

He says it almost matter-of-factly, as though he's

surprised that I would even ask. Maybe he doesn't realize how incredibly romantic he is. I roll him over and use my mouth and body to show him and by the time we finally finish, we are both floating once more on a cloud of bliss.

I start giggling out of nowhere and Flynn rolls over me and watches me for a moment, perplexed.

"What's so funny?" he asks.

I control myself and say, "Nothing, honey. I'm just happy."

I kiss his cheek and he settles in next to me, content.

I don't tell him, but the reason I was laughing is that I thought it was hilarious that I actually believed masturbating in the shower would take away my desire for him.

6

FLYNN

It is not strange for a dragon to become fixated on a woman. It is not strange at all for a dragon to become obsessed, in fact. I suppose any dragon will admit such a situation is actually very common, especially when that woman is immune to our charm and suggestion. In my life, the number of women who become the object of my fascination, fixation, and obsession number in the dozens.

But the situation with Mari is strange. It is most certainly not common.

This will make you judge me and will make you judge dragons in general but when we fixate on and become obsessed with a woman, we do so the way a human might fixate on a work of art or on a sports car. We fixate and obsess about the woman as a possession. We don't think of them as beings in their own right except in the way their personalities, quirks and emotions make them a more valuable possession.

Possession is not the right word because we do not think of women as inanimate objects. We do not think of them as things like gold coins or bars of silver. We do not think of them as creatures without agency or thought. Still, *possession* is the closest word to how we feel about them. They are something for us to collect and enjoy, something for us to add to our ever-growing piles of treasure. They are, in short, playthings for us to enjoy. Perhaps it is more accurate to say we think of them the way a human might think of a favored pet. We love them, but we don't see them as lifelong companions.

As I said, that will make you judge me.

You are judging me now.

Perhaps this will help ease your offense a little bit.

The situation with Mari is strange because I cannot think of her that way. Mari is not one of my treasures although I treasure her more than I can recall treasuring anything or anyone in all of the many decades of my life. Mari is a being unto herself, and I cannot possess her any more than I can possess a concept or a color. I cannot own this woman or count her as one of my baubles any more than I can own warmth or rain.

Mari is a force, a power. She is a state of being and she is the most captivating creature in all of my experience. When you consider just how vast that experience is, you can get a damned good idea of how highly I regard her.

Highly I regard her?

I love this woman.

No, that does not do the situation justice because I can count dozens of women I love over the years. No, it is so much more than that.

I am *in love* with this woman.

And I want her to spend the rest of my life with me.

My life.

And therein lies the problem. The rest of my life will be long enough to know ten generations of her descendants. Those humans who love her will mourn her passing for years or perhaps decades. I will mourn her passing for centuries.

There is one way to avoid that, but it hasn't happened in over a thousand years.

If she bears a dragon in her womb, her bond with me will strengthen and she will live for centuries and longer—enough to remain with me for my entire life.

I have said before that there are few of us. This is the reason for that. When a human woman bears a dragon's child, her life is locked to her partner's life. The same isn't true for male humans who impregnate female dragons. It only works when a woman carries a dragon's baby. As you can imagine, few humans relish the prospect of outliving everyone and possibly everything they love, so few women agree to this arrangement.

My mother, as far as I know, is the last human to enter this bond with a dragon.

There's another complicating factor. It is not so simple for a dragon shifter to impregnate a human as it is for a human to impregnate another human or another shifter to impregnate a human. I could have unprotected sex with her for the rest of her life and never get her pregnant.

Yet somehow, humans have born dragons. If only I knew how. I could ask my parents, but sadly, they passed on nearly a hundred years ago, having finally reached the end of the long lifespan afforded dragons and their mates.

I know no other dragons who have sired children.

I bank and dive steeply so I glide mere feet over the treetops as I head toward the small lake where I will drink and bask on the shore for a while before taking to the air again and flying back home.

There's no need for me to fly so stealthily. I am hundreds of miles from civilization in the unexplored wilderness of Central Canada and there's no chance of being discovered. I could soar as high as ten thousand feet without risking detection, but I choose to remain low over the treetops. I find it more exhilarating to navigate the changing terrain than to simply float where there are no obstacles to account for.

The need to focus on my environment helps the rest of my mind focus as well and as I beat my wings to crest a high ridge, then pull them inwards to dive back down over the other side, I come up with the beginnings of a plan.

It's not much of a plan, but as I mull it over in my head, I become more and more confident that it will work. I don't know if I have a right to this confidence or if I simply insist on it because the possibility that it won't work is too painful to consider, but as I land in front of my lake, I cry out in triumph and release a jet of flame that shoots nearly a thousand feet into the sky before dissipating into pure white smoke.

A dragon's flame is an interesting thing. The mechanics of it are fairly simple. We have two organs that sit just above our lungs that filter excess oxygen from the air we breathe and the water we drink and compresses it so it remains in liquid form. When we release the oxygen from those organs, it rapidly expands and interacts with the oxygen in the air until it combusts. It's a very simple design replicated by humans in flamethrowers and arc welders and rocket engines and many other applications.

What makes it interesting in the case of dragons is that it is very rarely used for anything other than a celebratory display like the one I show now. We don't use it to fight. Our flame burns hot enough to melt metal and turn sand into glass, but humans have weapons that could kill a dragon from many miles away and anyway, we're not at war with humans anymore. Dragons are immune to flame, so using it on each other would be equally pointless.

Still, even today when using flame as a weapon is pointless, every human depiction of dragons is of us engulfing people in flames. For a species whose entire evolution came about as a result of the manipulation of fire, humans are curiously terrified of it.

No matter. There are no humans to see me celebrate now. I release another jet of flame and take to the air, rapidly building up speed as I return home to try to enact my plan with Mari.

7

When I wake in the morning, Flynn is asleep in the bed next to me. That happens very rarely. I don't think he knows that I understand he spends most of his nights awake. I know about dragons not really needing sleep and only sleeping when they want to. Most of the legends take it for granted. The dragon always sleeps on his hoard but is awake every time the hero arrives? Clearly sleep is something they can choose to enter and exit at will.

It kind of thrills me when he sleeps, especially knowing he doesn't actually need it. I guess it makes me feel like he's completely comfortable and at ease with me and with our relationship.

It also thrills me because just getting to look at him while he sleeps is amazing. To see his muscular chest rise and fall with his breathing is a sublime thing. To see his face so peaceful and placid is like candy for my soul. Even while he sleeps, it is impossible to miss the very real and ever-present strength in his body, the power there.

And if I try to pretend there isn't something wonderful about regarding his cock, soft but still very large, as he sleeps, I think even the most imperceptive person will know I'm lying. In fact, it doesn't take long before my eyes stop traveling over his body and focus exclusively between his legs. It is amazing to me that after two and a half months with this man, I still hunger for him.

I guess I can't keep thinking of him as a man.

But what I fixate on at the moment definitely belongs to a man, a man I'm rapidly realizing is critical to my happiness and my hopes for a future of joy rather than... what's the word? Obscurity? In any case, I look at his cock and I want it. I want him.

And this is probably the main reason I feel a thrill when I wake, and he is asleep this morning. For some time, the thought of him waking to the feel of my mouth encircling his shaft enthralls me. When I fantasize about sex with him (and dear God, that happens all the time no matter how little time has passed since we actually had sex the last time!) I almost always fantasize about that scenario.

And now I can make it happen.

I move very carefully as I get between his legs and position myself. Although just staring at his cock from this perspective might be really enjoyable, I can't do it because he'll wake in a second just from my movement. I quickly lean forward and get my lips around him, thrilling at the feel of him in my mouth and moving my lips to get him toward the back of my tongue. Then, as I move my tongue along the underside of his shaft, I suck firmly and rhythmically. It's necessary for me to fight off a moan that will surely wake him as I feel him growing in my mouth.

God, it's like everything, every single little thing, that happens with Flynn is enough to make me react like I'm a porn star on camera!

He stirs as he sleeps and even that soft movement is enough to remind me of the sheer power he possesses. I wonder how it is that he can so completely belong to me when he is so far beyond not only me but every human alive.

I don't wonder for long, because the small gasps and sighs he makes as I move over him show me that he does belong to me and as powerful as he is, he is completely and utterly under my control now.

I have this thought often, I realize. I suppose I fixate on it because I keep waiting to wake up and realize that reality has reasserted itself and he is no longer interested in a lowly little creature like me.

He's in love with me.

It's strange to realize that as I bob up and down and moan over his shaft, moving my tongue sensually over, under and around him while still trying to modulate my actions to allow him to sleep as long as possible.

It's less strange to realize that I am also in love with him. Less strange first of all because I'm a fantasy dork and he's a dragon and what fantasy dork wouldn't fall in love with an honest-to-God dragon?

Less strange second of all because I realize I begin falling in love with him the moment I see him on top of that ridge right after watching him create the controlled burn with his fire. When he shifts to a human, I see the power and otherworldly strength, but I also see the vulnerability and compassion that I don't know if he even sees.

It's that quality that makes me love him. He is powerful enough that he doesn't need to be concerned with humans at all, yet he chooses a career that requires sixty hours a week of his time be spent rescuing humans in danger. He is ancient enough that no woman should be anything more than a diversion to him, yet the way he looks at me and talks to me shows me I mean more than anything else in the world to him.

He is a good and kind creature and the fact that he has the ability to be impossibly dangerous and terrifying yet chooses no to be only accentuates that goodness and kindness.

He gasps and cries out and I suck hard and fast, desperate to make his orgasm as powerful and long-lasting as possible. He wakes in the middle and when he sees me, he cries out again and says, "Oh God, Mari!"

I grin around his cock and keep sucking as he twitches and gasps and pulses until he cries out a third time and pushes me away.

"Oh God," he whispers.

I laugh and pull myself up to kiss his cheek. "Good morning, Flynn," I say.

He chuckles. "I should sleep more often," he says.

I giggle and say, "You should. That was fun."

He lifts himself onto his elbow and stares at me with the same wonder he expresses every time we're together. I smile up at him and say jokingly, "Yes? Can I help you?"

"Do you have any vacation time you can use?" he asks. "I'd like to take you on a trip with me."

"Hmm," I say. "Let me think. Yes."

He blinks a moment in confusion, then plays back

what I say and lights up into a huge grin that is so adorably boyish I laugh and pull him to me to kiss him.

That kiss, of course, quickly translates into something more and before I know it, his face is buried in between my legs and it's my turn to gasp and cry out and shudder.

If I thought I was good with my mouth, Flynn is god-like. I wonder if experience lends him that skill but decide not to ask him about that. Whatever he's done with other women, he is mine now and that's all that matters to me.

8

We are near the summit, but my conscience weighs so heavily on me I stop and turn around. "I want to marry you," I say.

She smiles but then the fact that my tone of voice is so obviously unhappy drains the smile from her face. "What's wrong?" she asks.

"I want to marry you and I love you," I say, "and I know this. I lived long before your ancestors knew there was such as place as North America. I lived long before your city, your state, and your country came into being. I have lived for so long it seems that one given decade blends into the next and I know that if I marry you, the years I spend with you will never fade. They will never blend into any other year. They will remain with me forever and will always be foremost in my mind."

She's confused and she smiles as she stares at my face. "Then why do you sound so forlorn?" she asks and then her smile disappears again. "Oh, Flynn," she whispers, "you'll be alone. You'll watch me grow old and die and…"

Amazingly, there isn't a trace of unhappiness in her about the fact of her own mortality. All of her sadness is reserved for the thought of my loneliness without her. That makes my love for her feel even more powerful and intense. I look at her in wonder and pull her to me, holding her tightly as she teeters on the brink of tears. "Oh, Flynn," she says again.

I push her back and say softly, "but there may be a way to extend our time together, to ensure we remain together." I look at the ground in shame and say, "I confess until we grew close to the time when such a way might be possible, I didn't think to ask your permission."

"I don't understand. Whatever it is, do it."

"I love you," I say.

"I love you, too," she replies, and I put up a hand to stop her.

"You don't understand. If we're successful, it means that you will live for centuries. All of your friends and family will pass away. You will see them grow old while you do not. Oh, it will be no matter at all to make them believe you are aging but I cannot possibly explain to you what you will feel seeing your loved ones grow old while you do not and—"

"You are my loved one," she says, "and I want to stay with you."

I stare at her for a long while and say, "It may not work. For more than a thousand years, it has happened with no human woman."

"What? What needs to happen."

"If you want to try this course and you are willing to be mother to a dragon…"

"Have your baby?" she asks in a voice filled with emotion, positive emotion.

I nod. "Unlike other shifters, we dragons are not so easily able to reproduce with non-dragons."

She smiles and says, "All I'm hearing is that we'll have a whole lot of sex."

I smile and say, "Yes. I have no doubt the time we spend together will be enjoyable."

She can sense my uncertainty and asks, "But?"

"But I don't know if it will work," I admit. "I'm taking you to the cave where I was born. My mother was a full human and she bore me for my father in this cave. I was conceived there as well."

"Is it like a magical cave?" she asks.

"It is sacred to dragons," I reply. "It is in my family's possession officially, but it is sacred to all dragons and all dragons who take a mate such as I am taking now visit here."

"So we'll see other dragons?" she asks.

"No," I say. "I was the last dragon shifter born, to my knowledge. There are others, but they don't show the same interest in finding a mate. I'm afraid we're a dying breed, Mari."

"Not if I have anything to say about it," she replies.

The fierceness in her voice is yet another reminder of how perfect this woman is and how fortunate I am to find her. I smile at her and say, "Yes. For a while, at least, dragons will live on."

She returns a bright smile of her own and kisses me softly. She takes my arm and we walk this way up to the cave.

When we enter, she gasps.

Few humans have actually seen a dragon's lair before.

It is a stunning sight. Not all lairs have a chamber filled with gold and jewels, but all are filled in some way or another with extravagant and valuable items. My father's cave is filled with sculptures. He was a great admirer of the Greek and Roman sculptors and the value of the ancient marblework he owned is likely greater than the value of the ret of the wealth we've accumulated. Of course, there are piles of gold and jewels as well. Three thousand years is enough time to accumulate vast amounts of many valuable things.

Aside from the sculptures, there are tapestries from ancient cultures from Babylon to Persia to Abyssinia to Mongolia to India, frescoes and paintings from antiquity to the Renaissance and many other priceless artifacts and treasures.

"I could get used to this," she says.

"It's yours," I say. "You will share all of this with me, whether or not you conceive."

"Why does it have to be here?" she asks. "Not that I'm complaining at all, but why here?"

"My father believed that there was old magic in this place. He and other dragons believe this was the place where the first half-dragon—what you call a dragon shifter—was conceived thousands of years before the rise of civilization. The legend is that a great dragon was wounded in a fight and nearly perished but was rescued from death and nourished to health in this very cave. He of course fell in love with the human woman who rescued him and, like me, lamented that he would outlive the love of his life. So, he poured some of his magic into her and she conceived a half-dragon, half-human child. Because of the mingling of their souls and bodies, she inherited the long life of a dragon and remained here with him for the next thousand years. They are alleged to have been buried underneath this mountain. My father believed us to be descendants of that first union. To be honest, I don't know if I believe it myself. Still, if there is a place where our union will be likely to conceive a child, it would be here."

"Wow," she says softly. "It's like a fairy tale."

I smile at her. "You'd be surprised how many fairy tales are based in fact."

My expression grows serious, and I say, "You don't need to do this, Mari. I love you and if you choose not to go through with this, I will love you no less. I will remain devoted to you your entire life and for the rest of mine after. Please don't feel you need to do this to earn my love."

"I love you too," she says, "And I don't feel love as a thing to be earned at all but freely given."

She steps forward and takes my hands in hers. "I freely give you my love, Flynn Aodh. And I want to do this. I will quit my job and stay here for the rest of my life if I have to, but I want this."

I lift her hands to my lips and kiss them tenderly. "Then let's begin."

9

If you do not have among your memories the knowledge of how it feels to make love on an embroidered silk cushion from antiquity somehow kept intact in the perfect environment of an essentially unspoiled cave, I can highly recommend it. When that cushion is also nestled in a pile of coins and gems that represents all by itself a fortune greater than that possessed by anyone on Earth but is only a portion of a much larger pile that represents more wealth, probably, than the collective wealth of all people on Earth; well, making love in those conditions is sublime.

Of course, you'll need a dragon to make that possible and even if you find a dragon, it's unlikely you'll find one as old and therefore as wealthy as Flynn.

And yet he is mine and he is above me, his cock delving deeply into me as I hold him and feel the pile of wealth shifting beneath the cushion with the power of our movements. Sometimes I wonder if it will always feel new to me. Each time he is inside of me, it feels like the first time. Every time he touches me if feels like the first time. When I touch him or kiss him or when my mouth moves hungrily on his shaft, it feels like the first time.

I don't only mean that in some romantic, melodramatic way. It feels that way not only emotionally but physically as well. It is almost like my body learns all over again what the sensations of penetration represent, as though I somehow progress from no knowledge at all about sex and sexual gratification to an understanding about pleasure growing and then orgasm exploding.

Every single damned time.

It's like I'm a virgin again but without any awkwardness or pain.

At the same time, the newness can't overcome the familiarity with Flynn and my love for him. As I hold him and we move together, I am not with a stranger. The sensations feel new, but the man does not. He is the man I love, the man I want, and the man who is literally my entire world now. For two days in the cave so far and for at least five more days after, he is my entire world. It is profoundly beautiful, and I am happy at the idea of him being my entire world forever.

I can't even begin to tell you about the strange and primal thrill I feel when I think about how he hunted for our food, leaving the cave in an immense blur of shimmering green and gold beauty, returning later with an enormous wild sheep and then shifting from the immensity of his dragon form to the less immense but no less perfect form of his humanity. My first tase of wild game only adds to the remarkable circumstances and only adds to my joy and desperate need for us to succeed. Oddly, the prospect of me getting to spend centuries with him is far less important to me as sparing him from centuries alone.

He cries out and I feel him pulsing inside me and I wrap my arms around him and hold him close, willing him to feel the love I have for him and take comfort in the knowledge that however long or short our time together, I am his—now and forever.

He holds me with equal fierceness and whispers over and over, "I love you. I love you."

I used to wonder at the monuments humans create to their dead loved ones. I mean, I understand an urn with ashes or a simple gravestone to remind one of the life that has left this world, but massive structures like the pyramids or the Taj Mahal seemed to me to be self-aggrandizing—a sign of their creators' massive egos and not a reflection of their love for another.

I know better now. When the love you feel for someone is beyond what you can explain or understand, you create a monument that is equally immense. I understand now how a king might be so devoted to his queen that when she passes he spends the rest of his life building a massive monument of sandstone and marble and precious gems.

I know now that if this is not successful and Flynn and I enjoy only these fleeting few decades together that my memory will be enshrined in something equally grand, if not as publicly visible.

When we are finished, I ask about that Taj Mahal. "Was he a dragon? The man who built it?" I ask.

He smiles. "No, he was just a man. A great man, but just a man. Does that surprise you?"

"I guess not," I ask. "I just... I can't wrap my head around us."

"What do you mean?" he asks.

"I mean the love we feel for each other seems to transcend time and space and life in general." I blush and say, "Maybe its silly and girlish of me to think this, but I feel like we are more than just ourselves—like our love was foretold or fulfills some prophecy or legend or something. I guess it just feels too powerful to be contained in only two people. Do you know what I mean?"

"I know exactly what you mean," he says. "And I agree. Our love is too much for both of us. We need a child. Not only to ensure you live as long as I do, but to ensure that we have an outlet for our love. I know that for humans, much of the joy of raising a child is the joy of knowing that the love they feel for one another is responsible for creating life of its own and that life can grow and expand past the limits imposed by the fragility and ephemerality of the lives who created it. It's how humans achieve immortality."

I laugh and say, "Flynn, you are wasted as a firefighter. I think you should be a poet. That was probably the most beautiful explanation of the desire to have kids that I've ever heard."

He laughs and says, "It is also a sign that you're ready."

"What are you talking about?" I reply. "I've been ready."

We fall into each other's arms again and soon I cry out as I am once more filled with his love.

We continue the same way for the entire week. We make love several times a day and when we don't make love, we just sit and talk. I feel so close to him. I am aware of the fantastic nature of this vacation. I am aware that this is like something out of a storybook, but to me it seems as intimate and loving as when my own parents would sit on the couch and chat about their day. Even the grandiose splendor of the cave seems homey to me by the end of the week.

I am certain of another thing by the end of our stay there.

Flynn's plan worked. I am pregnant.

10

I pace outside of the delivery room and try to remain calm. Mari is inside, tended to by the finest doctors in the world. I make sure of that weeks before, ensuring that the medical staff available to us when she gives birth is the best the world has to offer. The doctor is from the United States, the nursing staff from Japan, the midwife from Scotland and the technicians from Brazil. Fortunately, all our fluent in English, so there's no need to arrange a translator.

The pregnancy is simple and smooth without complications. Mari tolerates my almost overbearing helpfulness, following my diet plans and taking her vitamins as well as getting regular exercise and completing weekly checkups with her doctor. She thinks it's funny and endearing that I am so concerned with her but allows that I am more fearful than she is because this experience is new to me. This will be her first child, but she was present for her friend's pregnancy and knows more than I what to expect.

Today—the delivery day—begins with equal smoothness. Mari begins having contractions and when it's clear these contractions are labor and not the precursor Braxton-Higgs contractions, we rush to the hospital, and I coordinate with the medical staff I've hired to ensure everything is ready and waiting when we arrive.

Everything proceeds smoothly for several hours. Her contractions condense and her cervix dilates on schedule. She chooses to forgo the epidural because that can occasionally extend labor, so she is in some pain, but she manages it with her typical strength and resilience.

I call my friends from the company and those who aren't on duty come to visit. Brett, Rory, Stone and a few others wait outside the room and take bets on whether the child will look like me or like Mari. The consensus is that if there's any kindness in the world, the child will look like Mari. I understand the joke, but I find myself hoping the same thing. If the perfect expression of our love could look like the perfect object of my love, I could ask for nothing more in life.

Then there is a complication. The attending physician frowns and rechecks Mari's vitals. "Looks fine," he says in a tone that indicates that something, at least, is very much not fine.

"Is something wrong?" I ask.

He doesn't answer right away, and I repress a surge of anger at being ignored while the doctor checks the baby's vitals. When his lips purse, I know that something is wrong and I ask again, more forcefully, "What's wrong?"

"Mr. Aodh, I'm afraid I need to ask you to leave," he

says. "There is a complication with the child's heartbeat. It could be nothing, but it could be serious. I'm afraid we will need to conduct an emergency c-section."

I begin to ask for more information, but he continues, "That's all I know right now. I need to get this baby out of Mari and perform a full examination before I know more."

I hesitate until Mari lays her hand on me. "Go, Flynn," she says softly. "Everything will be okay. I know it."

There is fear on her face, but the confidence and certainty I see outweighs it and I leave after kissing her forehead.

Now that I am out of the room and it is over an hour later, that confidence has fled my mind and it is all I can do not to burst into the room and try to rescue my wife and child myself.

"She'll be fine, Flynn," Stone says reassuringly. "She's a tough girl and if that kid is yours, it's a tough kid, too."

"If?" Rory says, "What do you mean if? What are you trying to say?"

"Really?" Stone says. "Right now you want to make that joke?"

Rory lifts his hands and says, "Hey, you're the one making insinuations, not me."

I know they're joking for my benefit, trying to lighten the mood so I focus on something other than my panic, but I can't bring myself to be humorous right now. Brett notices that and says, "Hey guys, let's keep the humor out of this, okay?"

"Yeah," Rory says, "Sorry. I just don't want you to worry, Flynn."

"He's gonna worry," Brett replies. "He's having a kid. Everything could be nice and easy, and he'd still worry."

"Yeah, but everything will be fine," Stone insists. "These things happen all the time. The doctor is just being cautious."

He has no way of knowing that, of course, but I appreciate the effort he makes to reassure me. Unfortunately, the only thing that could reassure me right now is hearing my wife's voice and my baby's cry and knowing the two of them are safe.

The doctor opens the door and calls for me. My friends clap me on the shoulder and offer a few final words of encouragement as I enter the delivery room.

I walk inside as though in slow motion, my heart beating like a drum. When I see Mari open her eyes and smile at me, the relief that floods me is so powerful I nearly sink to my knees and the doctor has to wrap his arm around my shoulder to steady me.

"Hey, honey," Mari says.

Her voice is exhausted, but her face and smile glow with joy and love. My eyes widen and I say, "Is the baby—"

Then I hear that perfect little voice cry and I know deep inside my soul that I will never hear another sound so beautiful, so perfect, in my entire life.

Mari's smile widens and she lifts the tiny little bundle in her hands. "Flynn, meet your son, Aodhan."

I take the bundle in my arms and lift it closer. The newborn inside is impossibly small and I wonder how such a creature can even exist. It's so fragile and vulnerable.

Aodhan opens his eyes and looks at me and despite his tiny fragility, the strength in his eyes leaves no doubt about his nature. He is a dragon. He is my son.

And his mother will live for the rest of my life.

I look at Mari and smile. "We did it," I whisper.

She laughs softly and says, "We did. I love you, Flynn."

I return her smile and say, "I love you too, Mari."

I hand Aodhan back to her and one by one, our friends and Mari's family enter the room to meet him. My friends—normally loud and boisterous—are calm and almost reverent. They look at him with wonder and congratulate both of us in tone that a subject might use with a king and queen.

Of course, we are not royalty, nor do our stations—other than our extended lifespans and the sheer power I possess—make us better than they are. Perhaps they understand the momentous importance of the birth of a dragon. Perhaps they understand how important this is to me and Mari and they are overwhelmed with gratitude, as we are. Perhaps the birth of all life is sacred, and this is simply the tacit acknowledgment of that fact by the only species left remaining that understands that sanctity.

It doesn't matter. Whatever the reason, whatever the import, I have a family now. My wife will remain with me for centuries and my love will never want for an object. When our long lives finally come to an end, the purest expression of our love will live long after us, and the world will still know the power and majesty of dragons.

II

MARI

"Flynn, yes!" I cry out, shuddering underneath him as he thrusts powerfully into me.

He covers my mouth and I giggle in spite of the pleasure that courses through me. I forgot for a moment that Aodhan might hear us and wake.

This is the first night we are together since before he is born. The c-section requires a much longer recovery than a natural birth, and I think we both just kind of go crazy with the pent-up energy. This orgasm I feel now is the third orgasm so far and at the pace we're going, I'm pretty sure there will be several more before the night is over.

He moves his hand from my mouth to grip my ass and I bury my face in his shoulder to muffle the sounds of my continued moans and screams as he adjusts his angle to thrust deeper and harder into me.

God, it still seems like the first time. I am still overwhelmed by the godlike power of the man and the expert way in which he fills me with pleasure and sensation. At the same time, I am still amazed at the fact that I seem to be the one driving this. He is active and other than my hips, which grind crazily on him, or my limbs, which grip him tightly, I am the passive participant, simply receiving what Flynn gives me. At the same time, it is clear that this is for me and because of me and though Flynn takes what he wants, it is clear that I am giving more than he is receiving, at least as far as Flynn is concerned.

All of this is the same as it always is, the same as it always will be. What is different and new is the fact that there is no desperation in Flynn's movements, no urgency in his need to claim me. He moves with the same physicality, but the emotional energy of our actions lacks the fear and uncertainty of before.

We no longer wonder what the future will hold. We know exactly what it holds for us.

"God, Flynn!" I cry out as my orgasm hits again.

He too, cries out as his own climax hits and we hold each other, gasping and shaking, as our mutual climax affirms what we both already know.

We are one.

We are infinite.

A cry awakes us from our bliss, and we share a smile as we remember that we are no longer simply one in ourselves anymore, but one with the child we share. "Shall I feed him?" Flynn asks, his eyes brightening with excitement.

I laugh and caress his cheek. "Soon, my love. He still needs to breastfeed."

"For how much longer?" Flynn asks.

The disappointment in his voice is evident and the attempt he makes to hide it is so adorable, I laugh again, and this time kiss his cheek before rolling out of bed. "Just until his teeth start to come in," I say, "Any day now."

"Very well," he replies. "May I hold him when you're finished."

"No," I deadpan, "Absolutely not."

He stares at me in shock, and I manage to maintain my expression for several seconds before finally giggling.

He rolls his eyes and says, "You are a cruel woman, Mari."

"Maybe," I say, heading to the nursery with Flynn close behind. "What does it say about you that you fell in love with me?"

"That I am easily fooled," he quips.

"Can't argue with that," I say.

I reach the nursery and lift the crying Aodhan from his crib. He stops crying immediately when I pick him up and stares placidly at me, waiting patiently for his meal.

I smile at him and kiss his nose. He offers me one of those precious, open-mouthed baby smiles and I laugh and pull him close, embracing him before I settle in the rocking chair and prepare to feed him.

"He's beautiful," Flynn says in wonder.

He says that literally every time he sees Aodhan. I look at him and say with a smile, "You know, you got me pregnant so I could spend the rest of my life with you, but I think you love him more than you love me now."

"Yes," he says with a straight face. "Absolutely."

I look frankly at him and say, "You're really bad at this."

He chuckles and says, "Yes, deception is, unfortunately, one of the few talents I haven't mastered. It would be true, though, to say that I love you both equally. May I hold him now?"

I can't help but laugh at him. "Be patient, love. When he's done eating."

"Okay," he says, and looks so much like a child with his disappointed expression that I laugh again.

I laugh a lot these days.

Finally, Flynn gets his wish when Aodhan finishes eating and I allow Flynn to burp him. He holds Aodhan tenderly and his eyes never lose their rapturous expression.

It occurs to me that this may be the first time he's ever held an infant. I ask him and he nods in confirmation.

"I've been present for human births before," he says, "And for shifter births. I've never carried one, though. It never—well, this is the first time I've ever thought of an infant in this way."

"How do you mean?"

He colors. "I'm afraid you'll judge me if I answer."

"Why would I judge you?" I ask with a laugh.

He shrugs. "The lifespans of humans is at best measured in a few years compared to my own. Of shifters, perhaps a few more. Like I said earlier when I discussed the typical romances dragons have with women, we view humans and other shifters with the sort of affection we might feel for a pet. It's difficult to feel the kind of deep attachment a new life normally engenders when you know you will be present and virtually unchanged the day of that life's ending."

"I understand," I say softly.

I do. I recall how obsessed he was with ensuring I got pregnant and therefore lived his full lifespan. If he felt that way about everyone who ever lived and died, the responsibility and the pain of failure would break him. To someone who didn't know him, Flynn might seem cold, but to me, he seems almost intensely empathetic, so much so that he must create distance between himself and others to protect himself.

I walk to him and put my hand on his shoulder. "You don't have to hold back with us," I say. "Me and Aodhan —we will be here for as long as you are. He will be here longer."

"Yes," Flynn agrees. "Yes, I am not alone anymore."

"Never," I say.

I lean down to kiss him and that, of course, is the moment Aodhan decides to burp. My face screws up as I smell the sour-milk odor and this time it is Flynn's turn to laugh at my own embarrassment.

I join him in laughter a moment later and the three of us share a beautiful moment together. Flynn and I take turns holding and playing with Aodhan and Aodhan alternates between smiling and gurgling and regarding us with the perfectly serious expression babies adopt when they're learning of their environment.

We're a happy little family and knowing that I will watch this tiny baby grow to be a proud dragon like his father is the most perfect ending to a story that I could imagine.

12

MARI

"Are you ready for this?" he asks.

"Why wouldn't I be?" I ask.

He shrugs. "I don't know. I understand many humans are afraid of heights."

I smile at him. "I'm not one of them and even if I were, I could never be afraid with you."

He returns my smile and continues to strip. "Very well, then. I feel obligated to tell you that it is an incredible insult to ask a dragon if he or she can be ridden, but then, you are my wife, so if anyone has that right, it's you."

"Do you feel insulted?" I ask.

"No," he says, "Of course not."

He is so confused by my question that I decide not to tease him further and risk needing to explain everything I say. He finishes undressing and stands in front of me, tall and powerful and utterly handsome.

"Are you ready for this?" he asks again.

"I'm ready," I say.

"Very well," he replies.

I watch as he walks about fifty yards away, then shifts into his dragon form. When the transformation is complete, he turns to me and snorts. A plume of smoke jets from his nostrils and I smile and approach him.

When I lay my hand on his snout, I gasp. His skin feels as hard and smooth as polished marble. The edges of his scales feel like the facets of an enormous diamond. The power in this creature is so far beyond anything I've ever seen or experienced that I have no trouble understanding why dragons were considered to be avatars of the gods to many ancient cultures.

His eyes, however, remain the beautiful, sensitive eyes of the man I fell in love with. I gaze into those eyes and say, "Thank you," before climbing his neck and sitting where he describes earlier, in the notch between the last scale of his neck and the first of his back. I hold onto the scale in front of me and brace myself.

Then we lift off.

I am surprised because I expect there to be more of a sensation. I expect my head to be thrown backward, my arms and legs to slip and my body to struggle to remain upright and balanced as we tear through the sky.

There is none of that. Instead, we simply float away from the world. I am aware of our speed as the ground disappears below us, but I am not overwhelmed by it. I feel at peace. I feel safe. I float on a cloud of bliss and there is nothing but me and the man I love.

My dragon.

EPILOGUE

MARI

"Go ahead, Aodhan," I prod gently.

He looks back at me, eyes wide with trepidation. "I'm scared, Mommy."

"I know, little one," I reply, taking him into my arms. "But this is who you are. This is who you will always be."

He looks at the soaring form of his father, hundreds of feet above us, and frowns with uncertainty. He wants desperately to join him up there, I know. At the same time, he's never been off the ground under his own power before. He has no idea what to expect.

"Do you remember how it felt when your father first took you up there?" I ask.

He shakes his head. "I was too young."

"Well, I remember," I say. "You were two years old, half the age you are now. Your father came home from work and asked me if he could take you flying. I agreed to let you go if he agreed to let me come with you. He agreed, of course, and we went flying right here, right where we are now. I remember I was terrified of having you up here. All I could imagine was watching you get hurt, but when your father lifted off and I saw that joy and the wonder in your eyes as you soared through the skies for the first time, I knew that this was where you belonged. You're a dragon, Aodhan, one of only a few. This is your birthright."

I hold him at arms' length and say, "I have no doubt that you will be a great dragon one day, but this isn't about greatness today. Today, you're just having fun. If you just want to skim the treetops, that's fine. If you want to soar up to the clouds, that's fine too. If you want to follow your father wherever he goes, that's fine as well. Today is about you enjoying for the first time the gift you have as a dragon."

He watches me soberly for a moment, then breathes deeply. "I'm ready, Mommy."

I smile at him and kiss him on the forehead, then release him and say, "Fly away, Aodhan. I'll be waiting for you when you come back."

He smiles at me and looks so much like his father that I nearly burst into tears.

Then he shifts. It takes him a moment since he's not used to the movement yet, but soon he is a small—well, smaller—green and gold dragon—the spitting image of his father. He beats his wings and takes a running start, then with a cry, he lifts into the air. He hangs unsteadily a few feet above the ground, then, with a few more beats of his wings, he lifts off and heads to the sky, shouting in triumph.

I smile as I watch my son and husband soaring together and realize that I know now exactly what the stories mean when they say, "And they lived happily ever after."

DID you like *Deadly Dragon's Intense Infatuation*? I guess I'm more of a fantasy nerd than most girls because I really loved writing this book. I loved exploring a little bit about the idea of creatures so majestic they even make other shifters seem a little less supernatural. I have to admit, I kind of fell in love with Flynn, and I hope you did as well. As for Mira, I think I wrote her a lot like me. I'm just as scatterbrained and lost in my head all the time! I hope you enjoyed reading about their relationship and I hope you enjoyed that Mira ended up more than just a human woman with a shifter mate. Most people think of a twenty-five-year marriage as a tremendous accomplishment. Mira and her dragon shifter love will spend that many years and many, many, many more together. She and Flynn are in for a really happy happily ever after life and in their case, ever after is going to be a very, very long time.

There is more in the world of Company 417 to come!

How about something else that's wonderful? The Company 417 shifters aren't going anywhere. In the next book, you're in for an adventure. Tristan Knightly is a rare kind of shifter. He's a snow leopard, and there aren't many of them. It makes his human form talk, lithe, and Nordic with hair so blonde it's almost white. It's natural that when Cadence Elizabeth Rich serves him his coffee, she's instantly attracted. It's hard to avoid obsessing about him when the coffee shop is right across from the fire station. This firefighter is strong and dedicated, and when he notices her interest, he can't resist her charms. Their passionate first date exceeds all expectations but love is about more than sex. Tristan and Cadence Elizabeth will need to use more than their bodies to make things work. Sure, the date meant a night of passion neither of them will ever forget. It's an amazing start but what about what comes next? Can this hot beginning lead to another fireman shifter's happily ever after? Find out in *Sexy Snow Leopards New Love,* the next sexy and exciting tale in the always romantic and steamy *Company 417 Shifters* Series!